Timothy

The
Cornfield Mouse

For
Angela

William Fontana

The Chronicles of Timothy the

Field Mouse

Book Number 1

"Timothy the Cornfield Mouse"

Written and Illustrated by

William Fontana Sr. MA

2012

©2012 TXu 1-796-560

ISBN-13: 978-1493557240

ISBN-10: 1493557246

Credits and Acknowledgments

Cover illustration and art consultation by William Fontana Jr.

Proof Reading and many helpful suggestions by Barbara Minor

Agricultural Counseling and Corn farming information by Mark Foster

Very helpful websites: www.farmfreshtoyou.com www.wikipedia.org/
www.onthgreenfarms.com/fruit.../how-to-grow-organic-corn

Table of Contents

Once upon a time, there was a little girl named Amelia. She was one of the luckiest girls ever, because she got to live in a magical valley called Yosemite with her brother, Will, and her father.

Surrounded by high waterfalls and giant cliffs, this little girl lived with wildflowers, bears, deer, squirrels, butterflies, and many different kinds of birds, and oh!, lest I forget, there were *field mice also*. She learned to love nature. *And she wanted other little kids to be able to enjoy nature and take care of it as well.*

Since the time she was a very little girl, her parents, and sometimes her brother, read stories to her at night, right after prayers, and just before bed.

There was nothing little Amelia liked better than a good story right before bed. Usually, there were plenty of good books with great stories right there by her bed.

With her dad, this reading time had taken on a kind of ritual. Amelia would make herself comfortable in her bed. With her little girl eyes shining, she would hand her dad the desired book, and he would begin to read. After awhile, her dad would say "Well that's it for the night, goodnight Amelia." Amelia would say, "No! That's not it, just five more pages." Then her dad would say, "No, Amelia, one more page and that's it!" Then she would beg him "No, no, no Dad four more pages." This sort of a debate could go on for quite awhile, until Amelia and her Dad would come to an agreement on the number of pages yet to read for the night. And even then Amelia really hated for story time to end.

It is really hard to remember exactly when it all started, but it was during the normal reading ritual with her dad that *Timothy appeared for the first time.* There they were, in their customary positions, Dad in his chair, Amelia in her bed, and brother himself in his bed. The moon may have been full and shining through the mist of Yosemite Falls when it happened. Everything was in readiness for the nightly ritual of *story time* except for

one small detail….

Amelia's dad just sat there waiting for Mimi, as he called for her to hand him the book. Amelia was riffling furiously through her large stacks of books, trying to find a new story, but there was none to be found. Her dad was becoming more pleased with each passing moment, by the thought of getting out of story time and going to bed a little earlier that night. But for Amelia's dad to think he was going to get out of story time just because Amelia could not find her book was, how do we say, a little overly optimistic.

All of a sudden, Amelia sat up, straight as a board; there was a strange faraway look in her eyes. Almost, like an automaton, she held her hands out, and then turning slightly to the left, she bent over as if to grasp a new book. She picked up this book in her little hands, and with arms outstretched, she turned to face her father and very ceremoniously, placed the special book in his now outstretched waiting hands. And now I must say, to someone watching this strange ritual unfolding before their eyes, it would be very apparent that there was nothing in the hands of these two except thin air.

Her dad looked down and saw the title: *"Timothy the Cornfield Mouse,"* and began to read……

It was in a forest dark as night that little Timothy was born. There in his mouse burrow with his brothers and sisters, he would spend his mouseling days next to his mother, with the giant stalks of corn creating a magical dark forest of giant corn trees above him. When he wasn't trying to fill up on his mother's wonderful mouse milk, he was playing with his brothers and sisters in a world of perpetual night, at the

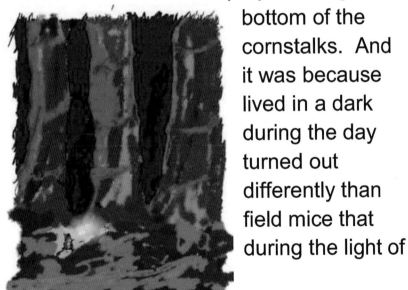

bottom of the cornstalks. And maybe it was because Timothy lived in a dark world during the day that he turned out differently than other field mice that sleep during the light of day.

Timothy quickly learned the skills of a field mouse. With each passing day he became faster at running, better at climbing, and more skillful at finding food for himself.

Timothy loved to play with his brothers and sisters. While he was having fun, Timothy also learned many skills and became a stronger field mouse.

At the bottom of the cornstalk forest, there was always plenty to eat. Timothy loved the sweet smell and taste of the corn stalks. And he loved to hunt for insects on the ground in his dark world at the bottom of the corn stalk forest.

From the beginning though, there was something very different about Timothy, or I should say, *quite a few things different about Timothy.* Timothy would stay up while his brothers and sisters slept in their burrow. He would take greater risks, and Timothy, unlike most mice who dread the light of day, was attracted to the magic of daylight. Oh, that is not to say that Timothy did not like the night as well, but the peculiar thing about Timothy, in mouse terms, was his attraction to sunny places.

Giant Leaf

Timothy loved to climb the tall corn stalk trees, and it was in climbing that Timothy made some of his first discoveries. Once Timothy was up in the corn stalks, his world changed rapidly. He found different kinds of insects to hunt for higher in the corn stalks, and there was a certain attraction in the giant corn stalk leaves. . .

You see, by climbing out on a corn stalk leaf, a mouse might find an insect to eat or an adventure to be experienced. Each leaf held its own charm and realm of possibilities.

Timothy climbed up the rough corn stalk about halfway up, and was pleased because his world was getting brighter. Then, there it was! *The biggest leaf Timothy had ever seen!*

Timothy was usually very cautious (something essential when you are only two inches long from the tip of your nose to the end of your tail and a potential meal for many different kinds of predators). He approached the giant leaf *very cautiously.* Using his wonderful sense of smell, he could tell that it was quite old. He also smelled something unusual on the leaf, which was *water.*

Normally, field mice do not have that great of vision, but here again (maybe because he was active in the daytime?), Timothy had great vision for a mouse. He looked out across the vast field created by the giant leaf, and there they were, like jewels sparkling in the sun: the water drops.

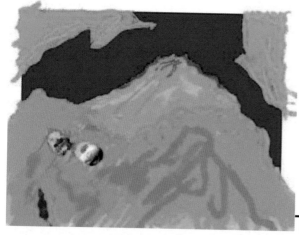

Timothy moved in little steps toward the grand drops of water. Then, he drank. With his mouse hands, he used the water to wash. He pushed some water on to the back of his little mouse head, and that felt so cool and good. Now, with his little mouse whiskers twitching, he moved further out on the leaf.

There were tiny green insects before him. He ate some of them. They tasted good to him, something like the corn stalks themselves.

Here, Timothy stopped to think, and again, Timothy was very good about using his mouse brain to assess danger and plan strategy, and actually this is something that field mice are normally quite good at. Something seemed perilous about going out farther on the leaf, but for the life of him, he could not figure it out what it was.

He could smell that the leaf was dryer farther out, and also harder and rougher. And that should mean that the leaf was more stable and easier to hold onto the further out he went. Should he venture out further, or just be happy with the water, food, and what he had learned and turn back to the security of the stalk?

Field mice are known for being wary (they have to be), but here again, as we will see in this story of the intrepid Timothy, this mouse was anything but *overly cautious.*

He ventured farther out, with the tiniest of mouse steps. His whiskers twitched very rapidly, his little nose worked furiously to find any change in the scent of the leaf that could indicate danger, but all seemed well. Little by little, he went on.

Then, it happened; he heard it first with his terrific mouse hearing (just the tiniest cracking sound). He felt just a little change in his footing; he could smell a difference in the leaf, but with everything happening so *fast,* he could not sort the events out.

He froze in place and waited, his little mouse whiskers twitching. He decided to return to the stalk. Slowly, he turned. Should he run back or creep?

He decided to run. He dug his mouse claws in for traction, and made his run.

As soon as he went, he saw the world about him turn upside down. As the end of the leaf broke, Timothy went tumbling down. His little mouse feet reached out for something (anything to stop his fall), but all of this had no effect. He was free-falling.

Timothy bounced and tumbled on the leaves lower on the stalk. Each of the lower leaves was braking his fall a little. He would spin; bounce, then fall, then tumble, bounce, and fall. After what seemed like a long time he landed on the dark ground under the corn stalks. He was upright and on his feet.

He was afraid at first, but then he thought; *that sure was fun. I want to do that again!*

Timothy, soon taught his brothers and sisters how to climb the corn stalks, walk to the edge of the leaf, then slide down and let the corn leaves serve as platforms to bounce from. And, I guess, it was at this time with his brothers and sisters playing this leaf bounce game, that Timothy first learned to love flight, because as this mouse fell and bounced, he felt like he was flying, *and he loved it!*

Ears of Corn

The game of climbing and bouncing meant that Timothy was spending more and more time above the ground, on the stalks of corn. He started to make some new discoveries.

He was climbing and looking for just the right leaf to fall and bounce from, when he smelled something exceedingly sweet. He edged closer. It seemed to his nose, whiskers, and eyes like a different kind of leaf, and yet there was something very strange about this new leaf. First of all, there were many of these new leaves together, and they seemed to be wrapped about something. Also, they were upright and not flat. Field mice are very curious animals, and Timothy just had to find out more about these leaves and the secret that they held. He climbed the leaves, and at the top, he found the most pleasant strands of translucent, moist strings. He smelled the sweet silk-like strings. He found that they had a sweet taste that reminded him of the color of yellow green. He then pushed away the beautiful strings at the top of the vertical leaves to find out what was inside.

For the first time, he saw the kernels of corn. They looked like little balls of yellow and white, and they were the sweetest smelling things he had ever sniffed. He just had to nibble at them, and when he did, he found they were sweet and delicious. Eating the sweet new kernels of corn made Timothy feel as though he had enough energy to be a super mouse, and soon, he would prove that in a way the corn kernels had changed him. Maybe, he wasn't going to be a super mouse, but as we will see, Timothy was going to do some very amazing things.

Great Flood

Timothy's mouse burrow was at the very bottom of the giant corn trees, and he had become used to the flood that every seven to ten days came in the low area between the corn tree trunks. The water would come down to the low area between the corn stalks, and then stand for awhile until it sank into the ground and was used by the corn trees. While the water was there, Timothy and the other mice would play along the edge of the water, finding insects to eat and sometimes crossing the shallow water walking on sticks and other cornfield debris. So Timothy always looked forward to the coming of the water, and the fun and opportunity that the water would bring.

This time, things would turn out differently though. It was just after he had found the lovely ears of corn, and enjoyed the sweet taste of their delicious kernels that it happened. He was playing as usual in the daytime, while his brothers, sisters, and his mouse mom slept in the burrow. He had ventured quite a ways from the burrow when his sensitive mouse ears heard it-----WATER. Then, he could smell it, and it made his whiskers quiver because he could tell the water was coming much faster and with much more force than usual.

Timothy was terrified! He thought of his mouse mother, brothers, and sisters, asleep in the burrow. He turned with all of his speed and ran for the burrow to awaken his sleeping mouse family.

When he reached the mouse burrow, he found the entrance blocked. His mother always covered the entrance to the mouse burrow to keep the mouselings safe from predators. By disguising their mouse odor with fresh twigs at the opening of the burrow, she hoped that predators would not smell her children. Timothy feverishly dug away at the barrier of twigs and fresh grass.

Just as he stuck his head in the burrow and squeaked a warning, the water hit him. He was swept against a corn stalk. He struggled to get back to the mouse burrow opening, but the water was too powerful (it swept him away, like a twig). He grabbed onto a corn tree and climbed for his life.

When he had time to stop and look down, he saw his mother, brothers and sisters all swimming and

floating away. There was nothing he could do, but watch them go with the flood water. They all disappeared so fast. He grew very sad, and wondered if he would ever see them again.

In the field mouse world, nature can bring changes so fast, but this was the first time Timothy would experience the force of water and the awesome power that it had to sweep away the past and change the future.

After the water went down, Timothy looked for his family. If only he could have found one of the members of his family, he would have felt better, because maybe then, he could believe that they had survived the great flood.

Each day, he went looking farther from the burrow, but at last, he had to give up and face life alone.

Golden World

After the great flood, Timothy was terrified that the water would return. He became more convinced that he should not sleep in the daytime, even though sometimes he became quite sleepy during the day. Timothy found himself spending more and more time climbing on the giant corn trees. He felt more secure above the ground. He missed playing on the corn leaves, as he had with his brothers and sisters. As the days passed, Timothy found contentment in searching for insects on the corn leaves and ears of corn.

The flood water never returned, and as time went on, Timothy started to play more on the ground at the bottom of the corn stalks. The ground became dryer and dryer. Timothy was becoming faster at racing over the dry ground between the corn stalks. One day, as he was speeding through the corn field in the dry bed that now lay between the corn stalks, he could smell the scent of another mouse. He followed the scent. He was hoping the mouse scent came from a member of his lost family.

He thought that he could see a mouse near a giant corn tree, but then it seemed to vanish. His heart was beating faster and faster, in hopes of finding a lost brother, sister or even his lost mother.

At the bottom of a giant corn tree, Timothy was sure the mouse scent went up the trunk, so Timothy began to climb as fast as he could. Up and up he went, climbing from leaf to leaf and over the ears of corn.

Then, something happened that had never happened to Timothy before, ---he climbed all the way to the top of the corn forest. When he looked out, he could hardly believe his eyes. As far as he could see lay a world of beautiful golden tassels.

He sniffed the wonderful scent of the tassels, wiggled his whiskers, and then lowered his head in reverence to the beautiful golden world he had found. The wind blew him back and forth on the tassel, where he rested as he rocked back and forth. It was if he was on a magic ship, drifting on a golden sea.

Then, he saw the other mouse. Like him, it was adrift in the golden sea. *Was it his lost bother?* Timothy called out, Brother, is that you! The other mouse answered, yes. Timothy now felt much better about everything.

For the next few days, Timothy had a great time playing and hunting with his brother. They often climbed the corn trees, just to swing back and forth, in the golden world at the top of the corn forest. They also renewed their game of falling and bouncing on the corn plant's leaves.

The leaves were changing though. Timothy's whole forest of corn plants was getting dryer and dryer, and sometimes rather than bounce the mice when they played, the leaves would snap, and break

Timothy had almost forgotten the great flood and was starting to sleep sometimes, during the day with his brother in their new mouse burrow deep in the corn field.

Terrible Machine

At the bottom of the corn stalks, the ground was becoming dryer and dryer, and more sunlight was reaching the base of the tall corn plants. Timothy could smell the change, the sweet smell of the corn was becoming dusty, and the once soft surface of the great corn trunks was becoming harder and harder.

One day, when Timothy and his brother were running and playing in the tall corn plants, they heard a very different sound. It was like a giant animal roar, but much lower and steady. The sound seemed to be getting louder and louder. In their whiskers they could feel the vibration. Whatever was making that awful noise was also shaking the very earth that they were standing on.

Timothy started to tremble with fear. He could not see the danger, but every part of him seemed to dread what was coming. Then, to his sensitive nose came a confusing mixture of scents.

There was the smell of the sweet corn stalks mixed with the smell of dust. But there was also a new smell. It was a strong and noxious odor that was entirely new to him.

He turned to talk to his brother, but his brother had disappeared. He searched for a place to hide; he ran into the mouse burrow, but inside the mouse burrow, he felt even more vulnerable than he had felt in the open. He left the burrow.

Remembering the great flood, Timothy decided to climb to safety. Up the corn stalk he climbed, over the leaves and ears of corn. He climbed a corn plant all the way to the golden world at the top.

When he reached the top of the golden world, he saw the terrible machine for the first time. The machine was a huge green beast that, with a great noise, came grinding toward him. He wanted to run and hide, but there was no place to go where the terrible machine would not find him and consume him as it seemed to consume everything in its path.

Timothy froze in fear as the enormous machine came closer and closer. The machine seemed to be drawing him in, like a giant magnet.

Timothy thought, should I run, should I jump, or should I stay where I am, in the hope it does not see me?

Freezing in place in the face of danger is instinctive to a young field mouse, or maybe it is taught to the young field mice by their mothers. However this response came about, Timothy chose to stay very still, hoping this monster would not see him, and therefore, not eat him, *as it seemed to be eating everything in front of it.*

All of his hope to escape vanished when the monster grabbed him and drew him in. He tried to run, but it was no use…

He was knocked down into a terrible whirl of steel and knives.

He soon realized that the monster was eating the ears of corn, *and not mice*. Timothy looked on in horror as whirling knives chopped off the ears of corn and then cut off the sweet kernels so they would fall into a collection hopper. Then, the horrible knives left everything else to fall out behind the great machine as silage.

Timothy had a choice to make. He could either remain frozen before the oncoming slashing knives, or he could try to jump over the jumbled mass of corn moving into the horrible toothed mouth of this monster. Timothy's first instinct was to freeze, but then he remembered what happened when he froze in place the last time.

It is hard to say, why Timothy chose to try to fly over the descending severed corn stalks that were being devoured by the great mechanical monster. Maybe it was his love of heights, or maybe that flying and bouncing game he played with his brothers and sisters, but whatever it was, you might say: "Timothy was prepared to take the chance."

Timothy took off like a bird. He ran and jumped over the descending jumble of cut corn. He could not remember what happened next.......

There was one last faltering jump, and then everything seemed to go black. Timothy wondered if he had passed into another world.

He dreamed of his mother, brothers, and sisters and bouncing on the big corn leaves. He made a leap of faith, knowing the big leaves would break his fall.

When Timothy woke up, he did not know where he was. He didn't know if it was day or night. All he knew was every muscle in his body seemed to be sore. He was very groggy, and very hungry. He must have been asleep for a very long time, buried in the wasteland of corn silage that used to be his wonderful corn forest.

After what seemed like a short time, but was probably a much longer time, Timothy dug his way out of the silage, in order to see what was left of the corn forest.

Wise Old Pheasant

There was nothing left! His little mouse body trembled in shock. Before him lay a new world that seemed entirely alien. The giant corn trees were all cut, their upper trunks lay strewn around in the open corn field. The lower severed trunks stood in neat rows, about two mouse lengths high. There were mounds of silage everywhere, like the one that he had dug his way out of.

Timothy was searching for answers. Was there anything left of his old world? Where were his family members? Where was the terrible machine? Was the machine going to attack again?

When field mice are confused and scared, they depend more on their ability to smell and their ability to sense their environment with their whiskers than anything else. Timothy tried to smell his way out of all of this. He ran in circles sniffing for new scents and rubbing his whiskers on the ground and the silage.

Gone were the odors of the terrible machine, and his whiskers only felt a kind of strange peace? There was much more sunlight in the mowed field than he was used to, but that only felt warm and good. *And yet, Timothy was as upset and confused as a field mouse can get.*

It was then that Timothy had a strange thought. Was this all some kind of strange mouse dream? Had it all really happened? Was his old world still somewhere, maybe, over there?

Timothy quit running in circles and took off in a straight line. He ran between the neat rows of severed corn; he jumped over the piles of silage. On and on he ran, hoping to find his old wonderful corn forest.

Then he saw it, and at the same time, he could smell and sense it with his whiskers. Something very different lay ahead, but what was it?

He entered the hedgerow almost without knowing it. It happened so fast. All of a sudden, he was in thick, green grass. It smelled moist and healthy. There was the sweet odor of many different kinds of plants and animals.

Timothy was really confused and lost! Obviously, his old world of giant corn trees did not exist here. Just as obviously, he had not been dreaming. Timothy needed help!

As often happens in the life of all living things, and especially little field mice, something seemed to be looking out for this little mouse, even in his darkest moments of despair and confusion.

At first he felt it with his whiskers, as they constantly twitched back and forth, then he could smell it, and finally, he stopped short, right in front of it.

He looked up and could hardly believe his little mouse eyes. It was both gigantic and beautiful. It stood there like a statue. Then it turned its magnificent head to the side and looked right at little Timothy.

At first, Timothy was terrified of this magnificent animal standing in front of him.

However, after all he had been through, and as confused as he was, he decided that maybe this animal, in its magnificence, *could help him to understand what had happened.*

He stood there very still and took a chance. *He talked to it.* As loud as he could, he yelled out, who are you? The magnificent animal threw its head back and said, "What are you yelling at, do think I am deaf? My ears are probably twice as good as yours."

Then, in a much softer voice Timothy said, "Please tell me who and what are you?" The animal then pecked the ground and made the sound that the wise old pheasant always makes before it begins to speak-- A clicking sound made three times, TLOT, TLOT, TLOT, and then he said, "I am the wise old pheasant."

Timothy, then said, "Can you help me?" "TLOT, TLOT, TLOT, Maybe I can," replied the wise old pheasant.

Timothy went on. He told the pheasant all that had happened to him. How he was so happy, then the great flood came and he lost his family. How in the golden world, he found his brother, and was happy again for awhile. And finally, about the nightmare of the terrible machine and how that machine almost ate him.

While Timothy went on, the great bird just pecked at things on the ground and listened. When Timothy was finished, the wise old pheasant answered, "TLOT, TLOT, TLOT, You are a lucky mouse, there must be a purpose to your mouse life."

Then he went on, "TLOT, TLOT, TLOT, Timothy you were born on a farm. The farm is kept by giants. The giants are very complicated. In some ways they seem very intelligent, in others they are blind. They mean you no ill.

The terrible machine is called a harvester. They were harvesting the ears of corn. They eat the corn like you do. You just got in the way.

Farm life, in fact life in general, goes on in circles or cycles. The farmer plants the field. The plants grow and the farmer harvests the plants. Our lives go along with those cycles.

You will learn, little mouse, what is taken from you, will be given back in another form. You must never look back. Always live in the present, looking forward.

You did the right thing by jumping at those knives in the harvester. If you had frozen or run, (as I am sure you were tempted to do) we would not be having this conversation now.

You are still Timothy the cornfield mouse, now go and don't look back, *live your cornfield mouse life to the fullest.*" And with that, the mighty bird turned away, and made three more clicks, TLOT, TLOT, TLOT. And then, Timothy heard a sound he had never heard before. As the wind beat him from the wise old pheasant's wings, the sound was like a thousand corn stalks blowing mightily in the powerful wind, as the wise old pheasant took off and flew away.

Timothy was dazed by the encounter, but somehow, he felt a lot better. He went back into the corn stubble field *feeling like a new mouse*.

Burrow in the Corn
Stubble Field

Timothy soon found a suitable place in the corn stubble field to make his burrow. He chose an area near the center of the field so that he could see or hear any predators that might approach through the dry corn stubble. He found cover in the corn stubble. He could run between the corn stubble and wind his way through it with great caution, so as not to be seen.

The corn stubble field was easy to hide in, but there was a problem with depending on the corn stubble for cover, as we shall soon find out.

Timothy learned to like his mowed corn field. There were many insects to hunt and eat, and the chewed up corn silage left by the terrible machine was sweet and good to eat, as well.

Timothy liked to climb the broken corn stalks and look out across his new world of corn stubble. He noticed, because of an uneven height of the severed corn stalks, that some areas were warmer and sunnier than others. Timothy liked to run through the field (all the while being careful to hide in the cover of the broken stalks).

He found that he liked the sunnier areas where it was warmer. He was attracted to these bright golden areas in the corn field. I guess you could say,

Timothy was reminded happily, by those sunny areas, of the *golden world at the top of the corn forest.*

Tunnels under the Silage

One day, as Timothy was exploring his corn stubble field, he noticed what looked like a mouse burrow hole. It even smelled like a mouse burrow, but more musty and moist, as if the mice had dug their burrow deeper in the ground.

Now mice whiskers have many uses, and one of those uses is to size up the size of a hole to see if the mouse can safely enter. Timothy put his head in the hole, and his whiskers did not brush the sides. It was okay to enter. He went in.

Inside it was dark and smelled musty. What mouse made this burrow? Why was it so big and long? Why did the mouse want such an extensive burrow?

Field mice are very inquisitive creatures, and Timothy was more inquisitive than most. He kept exploring. On and on he went. Farther, and farther, into what he thought was the grandest field mouse burrow he had ever found.

It became darker and darker, but Timothy forged on...then it happened. As the scent of a mouse got stronger, he heard something that made him jump back. *A voice*, "Who are you and what are you doing in my tunnels?"

Timothy could not see anything, it was too dark. Now he was a little frightened. He answered, "I am Timothy the cornfield mouse. Who are you?"

"I am a pocket gopher, and you have invaded my tunnels," was the reply.

Timothy asked, "You're not a mouse?"

"No! Most definitely I am not."

Timothy then asked, "Even though you are not a mouse can we be friends?"

The pocket gopher answered, "Why not, I don't believe that you want to eat me."

"No! Of course not," Timothy replied. "I am just interested in your great mouse burrow."

"This is a tunnel, not a mouse burrow! These are tunnels designed for finding food, and escaping predators," the pocket gopher said.

Timothy asked, "How do you find food in this absolute darkness?"

The gopher replied, "I smell it. When I have found roots to eat, I can eat them or chew them, and store them in the sides of my mouth.

Timothy then said, "I have never thought of storing food in my mouth." The pocket gopher replied, "You can't, you don't have pockets in the side of your mouth."

Timothy then wondered how this animal could find its way around these tunnels in the dark. The gopher said, without being asked, "I have a very good memory; I know where each tunnel goes."

Timothy was starting to really like his new friend, and also to believe he could learn something from him. Timothy asked, "Can you show me your burrow?" To which the gopher replied, *"The location of my burrow is secret."*

Timothy asked, "Why?" *The gopher replied, because it is a matter of life and death that only I know where it is."*

This all seemed very strange to Timothy, but he was happy to have the pocket gopher for a friend. *They touched noses in the rodent way of friendship,*

 and then Timothy followed his own scent back through the tunnels and out into the corn stubble field.

Timothy felt more confident when he left the tunnels, and he marked the opening to the cave with his scent. Having a new friend made Timothy feel less alone in the rodent world, even though his new friend technically wasn't a mouse.

Field Rat

Timothy would sleep in his burrow, then awaken, hunt for food and explore. One day, as he was working his way through the broken corn stubble field, he could smell the scent of a rodent. The scent was stronger than that of a field mouse. *His whiskers warned him to be very careful.*

He had just passed a clump of corn stubble when, out of the corner of his eye, he saw something move very rapidly toward him. He spun around and faced it!

It was the biggest mouse he had ever seen, and it did not look friendly. It stopped running at him and said in a sweet voice, "Hello, I am Willow, the friendly field rat."

The way that the rat had run at Timothy and the look in its eye made Timothy feel uneasy and tremble a bit. Something was very strange about this huge mouse.

Now, field rats are different, one from the other, just like all animals, and Timothy's worries about this field rat were correct. *Willow the field rat was a very dangerous animal.*

Willow was a predator rat. First, Willow would befriend field mice, then, when they were not looking, he would attack them in order to kill them and eat them. The only thing that had saved Timothy was the way he turned and faced the charging Willow.

Willow knew that even a field mouse could put up a good fight, and Willow (like all predators) *wanted to be absolutely sure of success without getting hurt himself. He would stalk Timothy to be sure of success,* and what better way to do that than to win his confidence first.

Timothy always felt uneasy when Willow watched him. And Willow spent a great deal of time watching and staying close to Timothy.

Normally, Timothy would go to sleep early in the evening and wake up before sunrise to hunt and explore, but with Willow staying so close to him, he decided to stay awake. The moon came up early that night and was very bright. Timothy liked the full moon because it reminded him of the bright sun in the daytime. To Timothy, the full moon in the night was like the bright sunny places that Timothy liked in the daylight. *For Timothy, the moon was the sunny place in the night sky.* He always liked the night better when the moon was full and bright.

Barn Owl

The barn owl liked the night sky with the full moon as well. With the full moon, it was brighter for the owl to see and to hunt.

I mentioned earlier that Timothy used the corn stubble to shield himself from the predators, and he was very careful to wend his way through the stubble so as not to be seen. I also mentioned, there was a problem with using the corn stubble as a shield from predators, *and the barn owl knew the problem.*

The barn owl has a dished face. The dish shapes of the bones in the owl's face collect sound. *The barn owl listens for prey animals and attacks by locating and following their sound.*

Although the corn stubble provides good cover from predators that use sight to locate prey animals, *an animal moving through a dry corn stubble field makes a lot of noise.* The owl was listening and watching from a tall tree in the hedgerow.

Timothy was looking for food and exploring, as usual, but because it was past his bedtime, he was getting sleepy. Willow knew this and was waiting for the little mouse to go to sleep so he could attack without the worry of a fight in which he could get scratched or hurt.

It was frustrating for Willow because it seemed to be taking forever for this Timothy mouse to get sleepy, but eventually Willow noticed the little mouse slowing down. Then the little mouse stopped and curled up; he was so sleepy, and the moon was so full and beautiful. *And he had completely forgotten about the field rat lurking in the shadows.*

WILLOW CHARGED! Timothy, startled, by the sudden sound of the breaking corn stubble, woke momentarily, but it was *too late.* Or, so it seemed. Well, it most definitely would have been the end of our little field mouse, but as the wise old pheasant said, *there must have been a purpose to his mouse life.*

The barn owl had been listening. She was confused by the sound. *There was one mouse, then two. One sound, then there were two.* Like all predators, she was patient; she did not want to make a mistake, *perhaps miss her target and injure herself in the process.* It seemed to her like either there was a very frantic and noisy mouse out there or there were two mice very close to one another.

She patiently waited for a single sound target. When Timothy finally fell asleep and Willow charged, *she had her single sound target.* Effortlessly, she let loose of the branch, spread her powerful wings, and flew like the wind.

Timothy squeaked in terror, as Willow pounced, sure that his little mouse life had ended. But then something very strange happened. Timothy was waiting to feel the tearing claws of the rat and his sharp teeth.

Instead, he jumped to his feet to hear and see the screaming Willow being lifted in the talons of the powerful barn owl. Timothy ran for his burrow.

When Timothy fell asleep in the comfort and shelter of his burrow, he was a wiser mouse. *He had learned many lessons on that moonlit night.*

He had learned to trust his inner feelings about strange animals who professed false friendship, and that at night the mighty owl, will take a noisy animal in a heartbeat. Timothy had learned to be a quieter mouse, especially at night in the moonlight.

Snake

The rest of that night, Timothy had bad dreams. He was being attacked by Willow, he was being hunted by the barn owl, and he was running on and on to escape. When he woke from his mouse dreams, it was early morning, and he still felt a little tired, but he wanted to go out and forage. He was hungry. Now, as he made his way through the corn stubble field, he moved more like a stealthy cat than a mouse. *He was very quiet.*

It was a cloudy day with some sunshine passing through the clouds in places. Timothy started to play a new game. He would run to the sunny places in order to feel the warm sun on his coat, and when the sun left, he would find another sunny place to play. He nibbled on silage and found insects along the way.

He did his best to run over bare ground, so as not to make noise by moving the broken corn stalks or silage. It is hard to say why Timothy got so sleepy. Maybe it was those nightmares the night before, maybe it was the sunny spot and the warmth of the sun on his mouse coat, but whatever it was, Timothy curled up in his favorite sunny place in the stubble field and fell asleep.

Who knows why Timothy felt secure sleeping on the ground in the open with the sun shining on his coat. Maybe, it was the fact that sleeping in the open the night before had in a way saved his life. Or maybe it was that he liked to be out in the daytime awake or asleep, or maybe he was just young and inexperienced, *but for a field mouse to lay out on the open ground in the daylight and go to sleep was not at all wise.*

Unknown to Timothy, close by another animal had been enjoying the warmth of the sun. This animal became faster and deadlier when its body was warm. Without the ability to heat its own body and blood, the animal depended on the warmth of the sun to warm itself.

When the gopher snake's body was nice and warm, it could move with great speed. It was a much faster predator when its body was warm.

Snakes are experts on body warmth, which is how they hunt. Their forked tongues can sense the warmth of other animals. They can also sense how the animals feels and if the animal is *awake or asleep.* The snake knew Timothy was *helpless and asleep*, and he could tell how close the little mouse was.

Not exactly where he was, mind you, but the snake knew the little mouse was very close. The snake moved very slowly so as not to make any noise or wake the sleeping field mouse. Closer and closer the snake came to the sleeping mouse. This mouse was going to be a delicious meal. The snake would strike like lightning and squeeze the life from the little mouse before it ate him.

Little Timothy's dreams were not good. He was being chased by Willow. His little feet were twitching as he dreamed. *Then it happened!*

Just as the snake was ready to strike, *a loud scream!* FOOLISH MOUSE, WAKEUP!

Timothy woke with a start, and since he was already running from Willow in his dream, he woke running, and the snake missed! Timothy saw the giant snake and ran for his life.

The snakes body and blood were warm, and it was slithering after Timothy nearly as fast as the little mouse could run. It was a lucky thing for Timothy that on that day, because of the cloud cover, the corn stubble field was not evenly warm, and as Timothy entered the cooler part of the field, his little mammal body just got warmer and he ran faster. The snake, on the other hand, could not go quite as fast across the cooler ground as its blood cooled.

Timothy's first instinct was to run for his burrow, but then he thought, "My burrow is so small, the snake will get me for sure." Timothy needed a bigger burrow to escape into.

He ran for the pocket gopher's tunnel. He found his scent mark and ran in. Yelling as he entered, "Help, help, a snake is chasing me."

When he found his friend, the gopher was digging feverishly. "Follow me," he said. *The pocket gopher had prepared for a snake attack.*

The gopher dug into his secret burrow and then he pushed the dirt over the hole. On the other side of the of the burrow wall, they could hear the powerful snake moving through the tunnel. They both waited in silence *(they were two trembling friends in the pocket gopher's secret burrow.)* Timothy now understood why the pocket gopher would not tell him the location of his burrow, and why the pocket gopher had said, "I must keep my burrow a secret, and it's a matter of life and death."

When they were sure the powerful snake had given up and left the tunnels, the gopher dug to the surface and let Timothy out.

"What are you going to do now?" Timothy asked the pocket gopher? The gopher replied, I must run to a new location and begin to make my tunnels all over. If I stay here, the snake will return, and next time, you may not be here to warn me.

They touched their warm mammal noses, and parted, closer friends than before. Timothy ran as fast as he could, but he did not know where he was going.

After what had happened with the snake, Timothy would never return to his burrow in the corn stubble field because he knew the snake would find him there. He had to find a new home. He also wondered who or what had saved his life by yelling, "Wake up you foolish mouse."

Again, Timothy needed answers. He headed for the hedgerow, wanting to find the wise old pheasant.

Covey of Quail

Just like the time before, Timothy was running so hard that he entered the hedgerow without even realizing he was there. He found himself surrounded in the hedgerow by birds. They were smaller than the wise old pheasant, but in a way, they reminded him of the wise old pheasant.

He froze, not knowing if these birds were predators or not. Would they see him? *More importantly, would they eat him?* The first sound that he heard really surprised him; it was his name spoken loudly and clearly, "Timothy."

One of the quail had said his name, and then things just got stranger in the midst of the covey of quail. After the first quail said his name, the second quail said, "What",

then the third quail said, "are," then the fourth quail said, "you," then the fifth quail said, "running," then the sixth quail said, "from?"

This covey of quail was talking in turn, as if they were one single bird. Timothy, no longer feeling ill at ease, answered, "From a giant snake." The birds went on pecking the ground around him as casual as could be and talking, each bird in his or her turn, *being careful to stay in their strange order.*

Timothy thought, if they know my name, they must know quite a bit more. So he asked them, "Where can I find the wise old pheasant?" In turn, they answered, "Look for him below the blackberry bush by the irrigation canal."

With that, there was an explosion of feathers and a call of, "TEEDEE, TEEDEE, TEEDEE," and the whole covey disappeared. Timothy was left alone.

Timothy was sure that if he knew what a blackberry bush and an irrigation canal were, he could find the wise old pheasant, but he didn't. He thought that they must not be in the corn stubble field, so he started walking away from his field.

Cindy Mouse

He hadn't gone far when he heard, *"Hey foolish mouse."* Timothy stopped and thought that; "that was the same kind of a yell" that he heard just in time to save him from the snake. "Where are you?" he asked?

"Well, I am not out in the open so the predators can find me," was the answer. "Where are you then?" he asked. "I am in the blackberry bush, safe from predators, unlike a silly little mouse I have been watching." Timothy thought, "If I can find the animal behind this voice, a least I will know what a blackberry bush is." Timothy then asked, "Are you the one that saved me from the snake?" "Yes," was the reply.

Timothy was confused and full of questions. Who was this? How had this animal watched him without his even knowing he was being watched? And where was this animal now?

All of his questions were answered at once. A mouse inched out of a thorny bush so he could see it. As they both stood there looking at each other with their whiskers twitching, she spoke first, "I am Cindy mouse."

"Hello, Cindy, thank you for saving my life," Timothy replied." Cindy did not reply. She just looked at him. Timothy wondered what would happen next. Finally, Cindy said, "Follow me," and she led him back through the underside of the blackberry bush and out the other side, where, for the first time, Timothy saw the irrigation ditch. And there, drinking some water was the wise old pheasant. The wise old pheasant looked at Timothy and Cindy, TLOT, TLOT, TLOT, he clucked three times, as he always did.

Timothy was the first to talk to him, *"Wise old pheasant I can't burrow in the corn field anymore. There are field rats, snakes, barn owls, and who knows what else trying to eat me.* Where can I burrow safely, he asked?"

Wise old pheasant looked at the two little field mice before him, then he clucked, TLOT, TLOT, TLOT, before he answered, "So you two have found each other,

I wondered how long it would take." The wise old pheasant then said, "*Timothy, Cindy is a good field mouse, stay with her, she will teach you and help*

you, but……." *And then in an explosion of flight, he was gone.*

Mouse Team

As soon as the wise old pheasant was gone, Cindy said, "Come on, foolish mouse follow me." Cindy then quickly ran into the blackberry thicket. Timothy followed her. Inside the thicket, she showed Timothy her burrow. It looked warm and comfortable. It was all lined with sweet-smelling dry grass and other treasures that Cindy had found. There was a piece of yarn, a shiny piece of metal, and some colorful rocks. *She had created a very nice-smelling and pretty burrow.*

She then told Timothy how she had watched him secretly for some time. She also scolded him for being so careless and carefree. She stopped calling him foolish though, but he could always tell that she was not happy with the way he led his life *(always looking for sunny places, adventure, and wanting to fly).*

Timothy took the advice of the wise old pheasant, and stayed with Cindy mouse, even though she was constantly chastising him for his careless ways. He tried to listen to her and make her pleased by being more careful, *and soon they were a mouse team.*

Timothy told Cindy the stories of his life, and she shared her stories with him. Timothy told Cindy about the giant corn forest where he was born, and was surprised to find out that Cindy was born there as well. He told her about being a mouseling with his family of brothers and sisters, about the fun and adventure of playing with the leaves of corn, about the great flood that took away his family, the discovery of the golden world, the terrible machine and his narrow escape. Let's just say, *Timothy shared his past with Cindy.*

She listened with great interest. Then she told Timothy her stories, and much to Timothy's surprise, Cindy had also grown up in the corn field. Although she had never climbed as high on the corn trees as he had, she had many things in common with Timothy. She grew up in the corn forest like him, she had learned by playing with her brothers and sisters like him, and she had barely escaped the flood, *but unlike Timothy, she had swum to safety rather than climb.*

There were things that Cindy mouse had done though, which were very different from Timothy, and *one of her stories really caught his interest. She talked about an animal that Timothy had never seen. She said the animal was a terrible red predator and that he had taken one of her brothers and that she had only narrowly escaped the terrible animal herself. She told Timothy that the terrible red animal was the reason that she could never forget the danger of predators and had to be so careful.*

Timothy and Cindy were together after that, all of the time. Soon they learned to work in the corn stubble field together as a mouse team. While one mouse would forage and hunt, the other mouse would watch for predators.

If there was a danger, the watch mouse would call a

warning, and both mice would flee or hide, depending on the kind of danger.

The days passed, and they got better, with each passing day, at working together. *I guess you could say, that Timothy became more like Cindy and Cindy became more like Timothy.* They were indeed a mouse team!

The mouse team realized that the predators usually were much faster than they were, *but not necessarily for a very short distance.* Therefore, they started to find places to hide and escape when warned, that were just a short distance from where they were foraging.

One time, when they were foraging as a team, Timothy remembered his mother and the way she used to place aromatic plants and just plain old twigs in front of the mouse burrow hole in order to disguise their mouse scent from predators. Timothy was thinking about this when he found himself next to the pocket gopher's hole where a long time ago (in mouse time), he had escaped the snake.

What he did next just seemed to come natural to him. *He started placing aromatic plant stems in front of the abandoned pocket gopher hole.* It felt good to do this, and it reminded him of his mother and his mouse family, *as he built what seemed like an unnecessary covering to a tunnel he would never use as a burrow.*

He was working, not thinking about Cindy mouse, when she caught him. She had ignored the pile of grass by the hole because it just looked like he was engaged in normal mouse foraging, but then she realized that this activity was out of the ordinary and really was a waste of time, considering that field mice normally do not do anything that is not directly related to eating, sleeping, tending young mice, or escaping predators.

Wow! When she understood exactly what he was doing she became very angry with Timothy. In an annoyed tone of voice, she asked him, what he was doing? When he explained that he was just putting grass and plants in front of the abandoned mouse burrow because it made him feel good, she could hardly contain herself. Then, she berated him severely. She said, "I believed that you had improved, and you were not as clueless as before, but now I see that you are a foolish mouse! What do you expect to accomplish here? How can you waste our time like this? *Do I need to tell you that while you are living in a daydream like this, I could be eaten by a predator?"* She went on and on.

Finally Timothy apologized, abandoned the collection by the gopher hole, and went back to foraging and watching, just like Cindy mouse wanted him to, *but he wasn't entirely happy, because he had enjoyed collecting twigs and concealing the opening to the gopher hole, and remembering his mouse mom and family, even though he knew in a way he was just playing around.*

Red Fox and the Magic Mouse

Timothy and Cindy did not realize it, *but they were being watched!* The red fox watching them was the very same terrible predator that Timothy had heard about from Cindy. The red fox has excellent eyesight (much better than most mice), and he had watched the mice from the hedgerow, and also from the edge of the stubble field. Like Willow, the field rat, he was waiting for just the right time to strike, and maybe just maybe, if his timing was good, he could *catch both mice at the same time.* Oh, what a wonderful mouse meal that would be! He watched and waited, waited and watched. He noticed that one of the mice seemed to be the more vigilant. Now, being good at strategy, like most predators are, he wanted to try and catch the more careful mouse first, and then he would be able to get the careless one and have a two mouse meal.

He knew his red color was a handicap in the yellow stubble field, so he stayed a ways off and waited for the light of day to be just right for his attack. He was very quiet as he stalked the mice. He would stay close to the ground and follow the taller stubble in order to stay concealed.

It was later in the day, the light of day was fading, and his red color would blend with the disappearing sunlight. He was getting closer, and closer to the two mice who were not aware that such danger was so close. Things were going very well for the terrible red predator, and surely, the two mice would have died on that day *if it were not for one small detail that the red fox had overlooked.*

The careless mouse, as the red fox thought of Timothy, was also a very brave mouse, and with a very brave field mouse, it can be difficult to predict exactly what they are going to do. This was one of those cases where the brave field mouse was more than a match for the *terrible red predator.*

Timothy was foraging, and Cindy was on guard. The red fox was getting closer and closer to Cindy. He was now close enough, to smell her mouse scent. He was close enough where one well-timed and accurate jump would give him mouse number one, and the second jump should give him mouse number two.

Timothy was tired of work. He wanted to play! He knew that if he was caught goofing off by Cindy, that could mean a great deal of disapproval on the part of Cindy mouse, so he decided to escape for a little while from Cindy. He knew that she was watching very carefully for predators, *but not so carefully for our little Timothy who was very tired of the drudgery of work.* So Timothy spotted a taller area of corn stubble and decided to quickly go to the other side of it, to see if he could find a taller stalk of stubble to climb and swing on for just a little while before she noticed. Timothy quickly ran through the stubble barrier to the other side.

When Timothy arrived there he got the surprise of his mouse life. *He was face to face with a giant red fox!* Maybe being so near to this animal was not as scary as the harvesting machine, but very, very, much the same.

Being a good team member, Timothy squeaked a warning to Cindy. Again, many thoughts ran through his mouse brain; run away, freeze, or do what he done when he had been attacked by the terrible machine. *He did the brave thing, the one thing the red fox did not count on.*

He charged the fox! The fox was so surprised that he hesitated, rather than bite the mouse. Timothy ran through his legs. The fox quickly recovered, but before he could turn completely around, Timothy was out in front of him.

Timothy knew he did not have much time before the fox would catch him. You might say his whole mouse life flashed in front of him. He was sure the end was near.

Then, while making his furious escape, the image of his mother came to him, and he remembered his collection by the gopher hole. He ran and jumped through the mound of grass and twigs he had playfully collected by the gopher hole.

The red fox was so close to catching the fleeing mouse that he could already taste a mouse meal.

Then it happened. *THE MOUSE JUST DISAPPEARED!*

Where had the mouse gone? *He was right in front of him; then, he just seemed to disappear into thin air. The fox sniffed the ground and the grass and twigs (unsure of his eyes at this point). No scent and no sight and no nothing of the mouse.*

And, this is when the legend of the magic mouse was born! The fox started to question his own judgment and abilities, but in the end, he developed a personal opinion that would not go away. HE HAD MET THE MAGIC MOUSE!

Farmhouse

Timothy waited for a long time, safe in the abandoned pocket gopher tunnel. It was very dark when Timothy made his way carefully through the corn stubble field to the burrow that he shared with Cindy.

Cindy mouse was not at all happy with Timothy. She told him how she was watching and heard him squeak. Then she saw the terrible red predator and was sure that he had caught Timothy.

She told Timothy how she had made her escape by running as hard as she could back to the safety of the burrow. She told Timothy how sad she felt at the thought of his unfortunate end, and she blamed him for not staying closer to her *so she could warn him.*

Timothy promised Cindy mouse to be more careful and stay closer to her so they could both watch for predators. *He was happy when she stopped chastising him and went to sleep.*

For the next few days, things went as usual in the corn stubble field. Cindy would watch, and he would forage, then he would watch, and Cindy would forage. But then something happened that would forever change their lives together.

They were close to the end to the corn stubble field when, for the first time, Timothy saw it. There it was, something that not only had they never seen before, but something they could have never imagined, *a farmhouse.*

It looked so strange. *It seemed like what Timothy was seeing was some kind of alien world.* He could have never have imagined something so different from his field. *He was fearful of this place, but at the same time, he was curious! Cindy, on the other hand, just wanted to leave this part of the field.*

Cindy told Timothy, we need to leave this area! This is the place of the giants. *The giants are fearful beasts who kill everything they see!*

Timothy could not explain why he was drawn to the farmhouse, but he was extremely curious. He told Cindy something that came as a surprise even to himself. *When she demanded that they leave, he said no!*

Timothy was sure that Cindy mouse would then leave without him, but that is not what happened. She stayed close to him as he moved closer to the farm house. *He then realized that Cindy liked him, even though they looked at the world in very different ways. He was grateful that she did not leave him, and together they moved closer to the farmhouse.*

House Cat

If Timothy had a problem in this world, I guess you could say he was overly curious! He ran through the gate to the house with Cindy in hot pursuit.

Once inside the yard of the house, he was unbelievably surprised. There were enough new things to amaze even a field mouse.

It was like Timothy and Cindy had dropped out of one world and entered another. This world looked, smelled, sounded, and even felt very different than anything they could have possibly imagined.

There were new odors, the smell of machines like the terrible machine, the smell of mowed grass, flowers, food, new plants and *animal odors.* As they scurried along, they saw machines, buildings, animals in cages, and animals that were free to roam. *Everything here in the farmyard was entirely new to Timothy and Cindy.*

When Timothy and Cindy went past the house, there were two animals asleep on the porch. They both looked like predators. One was a big animal with long golden hair, and the other was a smaller animal with soft black and white fur. They were curled up together and seemed to be sound asleep. Timothy hoped that they would stay that way.

Cindy and Timothy quickly hid in the flower garden where there was a wall of climbing sweet pea flowers, then behind it roses, daisies, tulips, daffodils, pansies, irises, Sweet Williams, and marigolds, all in neat rows. The garden was a wondrous place of beauty and fragrance. In the garden, Timothy saw honey bees, beautiful butterflies, and birds. He stopped to look at an Anna's hummingbird as it sucked nectar from an iris. Next to the golden world at the top of the cornfield, Timothy had never seen any place as beautiful as this farm flower garden.

Cindy was angered by the whole experience of being in this alien world of the farmhouse. She would have never entered this place if it wasn't for Timothy. But, she wanted to be a good team member, and she did not want to leave Timothy alone in the face of so many dangers. She was a good mouse at heart. She squeaked at Timothy to keep moving. *She was not at all happy with him just standing there, admiring a hummingbird.*

Timothy jumped when she squeaked, and started to run again. He ran for the cover of the plants in the vegetable garden. And, as soon as he was in the vegetable garden his wonder was renewed. What a place this was! There were neat rows of tomatoes, squash, radishes, lettuce, carrots, celery, and onions. The whole vegetable garden was surrounded by artichoke, rainbow rhubarb, and sunflower plants. There were also some grapevines in a neat row beside the vegetable garden. Timothy and Cindy ran and climbed over the plants. Timothy and Cindy even stopped and tasted some of the vegetable plants.

In the middle of the vegetable garden, there was a strange statue. It seemed to be covered in the clothing of one of the giants, but it was made of straw, like the straw of the stubble field. Timothy could smell, see, and hear the chickens and pigeons nearby in their cages.

Once they were at the end of the vegetable garden, they both saw something that made them freeze in their tracks. They looked in wonder at the huge animal. It was as big as one of the machines kept by the giants. Timothy and Cindy saw their first horse!

Then, as often happens in the life of a field mouse, the whole farmyard world changed in a heartbeat. First, a machine stopped a distance off. This woke the sleeping dog, and when the dog barked at the machine, the sleeping housecat woke as well.

Having two powerful predators wide awake certainly changed the farm yard world for the two field mice. Now, Sunny the golden retriever (a distant relative of the wolf), was mostly interested in the postman dropping off mail, but when the postman drove off, Sunny caught a scent (very faint) of a mouse, and as golden retrievers are wont to do, he followed his nose. Timothy and Cindy froze, hoping they would not be noticed, and noticed they probably never would have been, *but smelled, well that was a different story.*

Sunny moved quickly after the fresh scent of the two adventurous mice. Time was quickly running out for Timothy and Cindy. Cindy was now very sure they should have stayed out of the farm yard, but she also knew that they had a better chance to survive if they remained a team. *There was no time to chastise Timothy, only time to hope that the dog would not get them.*

Timothy, who was blessed with a calm spirit, did not panic. In fact, when he was in danger, he always experienced a strange calmness. And that was the case now. In the strange calm world that now surrounded Timothy, he thought that they needed a friend.

He looked quickly at the chickens and just could not bring himself to think of those strange birds in their dirty cages as potential friends. He looked at the pigeons in their cages, and they seemed far too nervous to be of much help. *He looked straight ahead at the huge horse. He could tell that of all the animals nearby, only the horse seemed perfectly calm and unconcerned with the dog. Also, aside from the giant form of the horse, the animal seemed to have a friendly disposition. Also, Timothy could sense with mouse intuition the huge animal was not a predator!*

He ran for the horse with Cindy right behind. Under the legs of the giant animal Timothy stopped with Cindy right next to him.   Starlight the horse brought her giant head down and sniffed at the mice under her legs.

Sunny, the golden retriever, by now had seen the mice and could not stop. Through the corral fence he went, at full speed. Starlight the horse had been with the Fontana family for a long time and because horses typically live longer than dogs, she had seen many dogs come and go. *She really didn't dislike Sunny, but she was not about to let any dog charge her at full speed.*

You can always tell when a horse is angry; their ears go back flat against their head, and sometimes they instinctively drop their head down. Starlight's head was already down from sniffing the mice, and when she saw Sunny running at her, her ears went flat against her head. Sunny failed to notice, and that was a serious mistake.

Starlight charged! Timothy and Cindy ran back the way they had come. Sunny forgot about the mice instantly, turned and ran, yelping as he went.

All of the commotion woke the sleeping housecat Patches (so named for the black and white patches of color in her fur). Patches watched the unfolding scene in a disinterested way, mainly just enjoying the motion as cats like to do. But, then, weren't those field mice that were running into the flower garden?

Patches was up in a second and running after the mice. Timothy knew that they did not have a chance if they tried to outrun the pursuing cat. *Again, Timothy became very calm inside; it was almost as if he were in another place, not in a farmyard, running for his life from the deadly house cat.*

In his special calm place he thought, I am not going to let the house cat kill us both. He told Cindy, "Run for your life and don't look back!" And that's exactly what she did.

Timothy, on the other hand, slowed down and climbed up into the wall of sweet pea flowers. *If it wasn't for the fact that the house cat was trying to kill him,* he could have really enjoyed spending some time, and perhaps playing, in this amazing pink world of fragrant flowers.

The cat stopped, and with its big green eyes, looked up into the pink world of flowers in front of her. She wondered, "Now where is that delicious field mouse? I know he's in there somewhere."

Patches really wasn't a vicious predator. She actually was a well-fed housecat, with a bell collar around her neck (to keep her from killing birds). That having been said, *she would have gladly caught Timothy, killed and ate him.*

By now though, Timothy had spent a lot of time in his special reality that only existed when his life was *in extreme danger.* And somehow, don't ask me how, Timothy noticed that there was a big difference between Patches, and say, the terrible red predator, or Willow the field rat for that matter. *He sensed (maybe with his special mouse whiskers) that Patches wanted to play as much as she wanted to kill him. Timothy loved to play as well. So, that's how it started the amazing "sweet pea flower cat and mouse game."*

Timothy would climb carefully through the flower bush, and then he would violently shake the internal branches of the flower bush. The cat would move to the area of new motion each time and remain transfixed, watching the pretty flowers move. This went on for quite awhile with both the cat and the mouse having quite a bit of fun. *Then, Timothy became very tired and decided he really did need to stop playing and try to escape.*

He climbed high up into the left side of the flower bush, and then shook the branches. The housecat dutifully moved to the left. Timothy quietly dropped to the ground inside the flower bush and escaped, walking *very slowly* (not running because by now he knew how much Patches loved motion), right behind the cat, out of the right side of the flower bush.

When he was safely in the corn stubble field, he ran like crazy back to the hedge row, to Cindy and his burrow.

Jasper the Jackrabbit

When Timothy returned to the burrow, Cindy was so glad to see him that she jumped all over the place and ran around in circles (as mice do when they are really excited). She told Timothy that she was so grateful that they were both alive and that she would never return to that horrible world of the farmhouse!

Timothy, on the other hand, was excited and even more curious about the world of the farmhouse, and, at the same time, he shared Cindy's trepidation about returning. Would he ever go back, or more importantly, without Cindy, would he ever be able to go back to the farmhouse?

A strange thing had happened to Timothy in the world of the farmhouse. He had learned that there was a different class of animals. The animals that he had found there were kind of in between the wild animals of the cornfield and something else. What was the something else? The something else caused him to wonder, and if you are Timothy the cornfield mouse, wonder you must!

Of all of the things that happened to Timothy in the farmyard that caused him to wonder, he thought mostly of the horse (that huge animal that had saved his life). There was something *fundamentally different* about that animal, and Timothy intended to find out what it was.

One day, when Timothy and Cindy were foraging and watching out for each other in the corn stubble field, something happened that taught Timothy a great deal. What it was, was an incident that would lead to another incident, and then another, and on and on, but isn't that the way we learn all new things?

Timothy was getting bored of just foraging and wanted to play. He really shouldn't have done it, but he did. He started running back and forth as fast as he could, just to enjoy the speed and the way the wind pushed on his fur and whiskers. He had just made one of his lightning-like turns and was at about his top mouse speed, when right beside him, was another animal who also loved to run for the fun of it. It was Jasper the jackrabbit. This may have been the only time in history that a fully fledged race occurred between a field mouse and a jackrabbit.

Young Jasper loved to run!

Timothy barely had time to consider; whether his racing partner was a predator and will this be the last time I mess around when I should be working? When Jasper outdistanced Timothy, all he could do was to watch in utter amazement as Jasper bounded off in the distance. All he could see after a very short time were the tips of two long ears disappearing in the distance, and he knew one thing for sure: that this animal was *no predator.*

Timothy could not help himself but be very curious about the rabbit. How could an animal run that fast?

It was a strange thought, but in some way, that rapid animal reminded him of Starlight the horse. Was there a connection between Jasper and Starlight, and if so what was it?

Of course Cindy was very upset with Timothy for racing the jackrabbit, but Timothy made up his mind to find out more about that fantastic runner.

It was sometime later, in the hedgerow, that Timothy saw Jasper eating fresh young shoots of grass. He was so excited about seeing that fantastic running animal that he trembled. His whiskers twitched, he tried to smell the animal. He crept closer, and closer, afraid that at any moment, the rabbit would explode into an unbelievable amount of velocity. He wanted to learn more about this animal. He had many questions.

The animal did not explode into pure velocity. He just nibbled on the fresh shoots of grass and calmly looked at Timothy.

"What's going on, little mouse? Do you want to race again?" *Timothy quickly answered, "No."*

He just stood there, looking at the rabbit that seemed so big compared to him. Finally, thinking that this animal might be some kind of a large mouse with very long ears, he asked the rabbit "Are you looking for plants and insects to eat?"

The rabbit quickly picked up its head. "What! Did you say insects?" Timothy replied, "Yes."

Jasper then said, "Insects?! how disgusting! I would not be caught dead eating insects, I eat on*ly plants.*"

Timothy, then asked, "You're not a predator are you?" Jasper replied, "Heavens no, I hate predators!" Timothy then asked, "Is that why you are so fast?" To which the rabbit answered, "Definitely yes! Predators can eat my dust!" And with that, Jasper bounded off.

Timothy watched him go, and then again he began to wonder about the connection between the rabbit and Starlight the horse. Maybe, he thought, the horse only eats plant food as well. After all, the horse was not a predator and also very fast; he sure made that dog run. It was at this point that Timothy realized that even though he was different from the horse and the rabbit in what he ate, he had affection for these fast large animals that only ate plants. Among all of the larger animals that he had met, to this point in his life, they were the only ones that did not want to eat him!

Grey World

The corn stubble field was getting dryer and dryer, and there was less for the mice to find to eat, so they were ranging farther, and farther, in the field to find food. On one of their forays, they reached the end of the field. At the end of the corn stubble field, they could have gone back into the farm yard or explored the grey world, and because Cindy refused to return to the farmyard, they chose to follow the grey asphalt road. The mice thought that there might be something to eat alongside it. They found broken bottles, candy wrappers, old hubcaps, and many other strange things, but nothing to eat. *It was a world of grey with colored powerful machines that whizzed by.* The machines made a horrible noise as they went speeding by. Timothy and Cindy could smell the acrid odor the machines made, and the terrible noise hurt their ears, but they were hungry so they pushed on.

They had gone a ways without finding any food when it occurred to Timothy that they might do better on the other side of the road. It didn't seem that far to cross the road, and the machines only passed occasionally.

Something happened though, that would change the way the mice viewed the grey world forever. Alongside of the road, there was a rabbit that was also looking for a better place to forage. The rabbit seemed tense and nervous about crossing the road. Timothy wondered why. He watched the rabbit to see how he would cross the road.

The noise and the smell were terrible when the rabbit ran. Then Timothy saw something that would change his mind forever regarding the grey world.

One of the machines hit the running rabbit. The poor animal cried out, and then tumbled over and over to the other side of the road.

When the animal got up and limped away, Timothy knew that it had been hurt badly. Why had the machine not stopped? If it was a predator, it would have stopped to kill the rabbit. He remembered the terrible machine and what the wise old pheasant had told him about the giants, (the giants are complicated. In some ways they are very intelligent in other ways they are blind). Timothy and Cindy left the grey world. *Timothy never wanted to return to the grey world again, but he knew that if he did, he would have to figure out a way to not get run down by the speeding machines.*

Fire!

After foraging in the corn stubble field and the grey world, the hedgerow was looking better and better. When Timothy and Cindy returned to the hedgerow, they were tired and still a little hungry. Timothy was not at all anxious to return to foraging in the corn stubble field *and certainly had no intention to return to the grey world.* In the hedgerow, the plants were still growing because of the water from the irrigation ditch, and there were more insects there as well. Also, the giants hardly ever came to the hedge row, and the hedgerow was never harvested so the mice did not have to worry about machines in the hedgerow. It was a place of refuge for the wild animals that lived on the farm.

Because of the drying corn stubble field, the field mice were barely able to sustain themselves. They were only able to survive by foraging in the hedgerow. Timothy and Cindy were about to abandon the farm in search of a better place to forage when it happened!

The first thing that Timothy sensed was the smell of smoke. Then he heard the loud talking of the giants. After he climbed higher in the blackberry bush and peered out, he could see what was happening. *There was a line of fire all of the way across the corn stubble field.* The giants had set the corn stubble field on fire. Timothy and Cindy did not know what to do, but instinctively, Cindy and Timothy (like all field mice) were both terrified of fire.

Timothy wondered about the field mouse options in the face of this powerful fire. They could run, stay in place, or hide. Timothy decided they should flee the advancing fire.

They had not gone far when they saw many animals hiding by the irrigation ditch, and one of them was the wise old pheasant. Both Timothy and Cindy ran down to where the wise old pheasant was hiding. They thought that it would be safer near the wise bird, and also, maybe, the wise old pheasant knew more about this fire, and could help them to understand what was going on.

The wise old pheasant was not at all happy about the field mice approaching him when he was trying to hide. TLOT, TLOT, TLOT, he told them to never approach him again when he was hiding. *He explained that for him, hiding successfully meant survival. He told Timothy that, if a predator followed the scent of the mice, his hiding place could be found. He also told the two mice that, he had special hiding places that he favored, like this one in the tall grass by the irrigation ditch, and it was important to keep his special hiding places a secret.*

Timothy and Cindy listened patiently, and then, they asked the wise old pheasant, *"What is happening?"*

The wise old pheasant said, "The giants are burning the corn field so they can plant a new type of plant in the field." He told them that, the fire would make the ground healthier for the new plants. The fire would kill the insects, diseases, and make the ground richer in plant foods for the new plants that the giants would surely plant soon.

He also, told them that, the giants only wanted to burn the corn stubble field, and that they were able to control the fire, so they would be safe as long as they stayed in the hedge row. The wise old pheasant then said something that surprised the mice. He told them that, *they could hide beside him, near the irrigation ditch in the tall grass.* Cindy and Timothy quickly went into the tall grass next to the wise old pheasant, where on that special day of smoke and fire, *somewhere in the San Joaquin Valley on a small family-owned organic farm, two little field mouse were snuggled up next to a Chinese ring-necked pheasant where no one could find them, while fire raged through the corn stubble field.*

At this point in the story, Amelia sat up ramrod straight in her bed, with a faraway look in her eyes. "Daddy, she said, it is time for a new book." Her dad put his hands together, as if to close the imaginary book. He reached over and handed it to her. She very carefully took the book and placed it on her bookshelf. Then, as if to look for a new book, she went through some books and finally said, "Oh! There it is!" Then, she held her arms out to her left side, and, turning to her right, she carefully placed the new book in her father's outstretched waiting hands.

Her dad looked down and saw the title, *"Timothy the Tomato Field Mouse."*

Made in the USA
Charleston, SC
26 October 2014